Bunny Rabbit Rebus

by David A. Adler
Pictures by
Madelaine Gill Linden

Puffin Books

To Uncle Walter and Aunt Hilda

PUFFIN BOOKS

Viking Penguin Inc., 40 West 23rd Street, New York, New York, 10010, U.S.A.
Penguin Books Ltd, Harmondsworth, Middlesex, England
Penguin Books Australia Ltd, Ringwood, Victoria, Australia
Penguin Books Canada Limited, 2801 John Street, Markham, Ontario, Canada L3R 1B4
Penguin Books (N.Z.) Ltd, 182–190 Wairau Road, Auckland 10, New Zealand

First published by Thomas Y. Crowell, 1983
Published in Picture Puffins 1987
Text copyright © David A. Adler, 1983
Illustrations copyright © Madelaine Gill Linden, 1983
All rights reserved
Printed in Japan by Dai Nippon Printing Co. Ltd.
Set in Galliard.

Library of Congress catalog card number: 86-43221
ISBN 0-14-050775-2

Bunny Rabbit Rebus

This is Little Rabbit. This is Mother Rabbit. And this is their story.

In this Bunny Rabbit Rebus, some of the words, or parts of words, have been replaced with pictures. A word spelled with pictures is called a rebus.

Some of the rebus words will be easy to read. is lettuce. is rabbit. is feathers.

Some of the rebuses will not be so easy to read. 4 is before, E is ready, and ld is told.

If you read the story slowly, you should be able to read every word. But if you miss some, you can look in the glossary on pages 30-31. The story without rebuses begins on page 32.

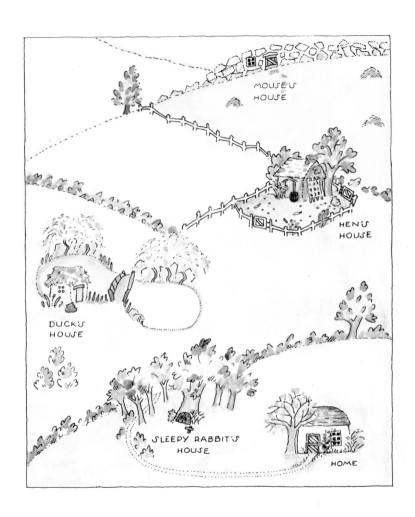

MOUSE'S HOUSE

HEN'S HOUSE

DUCK'S HOUSE

SLEEPY RABBIT'S HOUSE

HOME

"👁'm hungry. 👁'm hungry," 🐰 told his mother. "👁 want something 2 eat."

🐰 looked 4 some 🥕🍎 2 give 2 🐰. She looked on the 🪑, but the 🪑 was 🐹.

"👁 thought 👁 had some 🥕 h..."

🐞 said. "Did U C them?"

"👁 8 them," 🐞 told her.

🐞 o/ed the 🌳🚪 . She looked on the 🥕 shelf.

"👁 was sure 👁 had some 🌱 h❄ ."

"U did," 🐞 said. "But 👁 8 it."

"O 🧱 ," 🐞 said. "👁 shall look in m👁 Ccret place. There is always a 🥕 or 2 there 4 a hungry little 🐰 ."

🐞 cl👁mbed on a 🪑 . She o/ed the ☕ . She reached 🖐h👁nd some 🍪🍪🍪

and took out a yellow 🧺 . The 🧺
was MT.

"Did U eat these 🥕 2?" 🐰 asked.

🐰 nodded his 👂 . "👁 cl👁mbed up and
found them," he said.

🐰 got down from the 🪑 . "U've
E 10 everything," she said. "🧱 then,
🎡 just have 2 get some more. Let's go
2 Sleepy 🐰 and ask him 4 some 🫛
and 🥕."

🐰 and 🐰 walked down the 🪜 2

Sleepy 🐰's 🏠. They found Sleepy 🐰 outs👁de, resting on a 🛏.

"Who's there?" Sleepy 🐰 asked. He sat up and rubbed his 👁 👁. "Who woke me from m👁 nap?"

"It's me. It's 🐰. 🐰 is hungry. 🥫 U give him some 🍵 or 🌾 2 eat?"

"What! First U wake me from m👁 nap. Now U ask me 2 feed 🐰. Wh👁 should 👁?"

"👁'm sorry we woke U," 🐰 said,

and she ☆ted 2 leave.

"No. W8," Sleepy 🐰 called out. "👁 🐜d something 2. My 🛏 🐜ds more 🥚🥚🥚. If U get me some 🥚🥚🥚, 👁'll give 🐿 🌾🌾🌾 and 🐑."

"Come with me," 🐰 🐑ld 🐿. "Let's go 2 🦆's 🏠. May🐝 🦆 will give us some 🥚🥚🥚."

🐰 and 🐿 walked 2 🦆's 🏠. 🦆 was outs👁de, loo🐛 up at the sk👁.

"Do U th🍼 it will 🌧 ?" 🦆 asked.

"👁'm all out of ☁water."

🐰 and 🐝 looked up 2. "👁 C some ☁☁ just 🐝yond the 🌳," 🐰 said. "It might ☁ later in the day."

When 🦆 s🥕ped loo🦊 at the sk👁, 🐰 🦾ld her, "🦊 is hungry. Sleepy 🐰 said he 🪵 give us some 🐢 and 🌱 if 👁 🪵 give him some 🥚🥚🥚. Do U have some 🥚🥚🥚 that U 🥫 give me 4 Sleepy 🐰?"

"Take all the 🥚🥚🥚 U want," 🦆 said.

"They're all over the 🏠. They 🔑p falling out."

🐰 and 🐥 collected a big 🥧le of 🥚🥚🥚. They ⭐ted 2 leave.

"W8," 🦆 called. "🥫 U get me something 2 collect ☁water? All 👁 have is this small 🎀l."

"🐔 has an MT 🛢," 🐰 said. "May🐝 she'll give it 2 me."

🐰 ran off 2 🐔's 🏠. Some of the 🥚🥚🥚 she was 🔨lding flew in2 the air.

did s 2 them up.

ted 2 follow his mother.

", ," called out. "Don't run

off. said U were hungry. have a

le of :,. Wh don't U eat some.'

8 1 ful of :, after the other.

finally sped him. "U've had

enough," she said.

ed up some of the that had

fallen. Then he ran 2 's . was

alE there. was sweeping the

floor with a .

  When ished sweeping, ld , " is hungry. Sleepy said he give us some and if give him some . gave me the but she wants a . Do have a that could give me 4 ?"

  " take the b the ," said.

  put the she had insde the . put the he was lding in

the 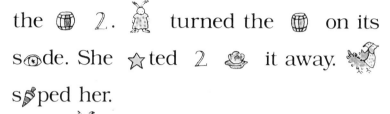 2. turned the on its
s⊙de. She ☆ted 2 it away.
s⟋ped her.

"O ," she called. "There's
something ⊙ ⌐d. U get me some
fresh 4 m⊙ ?"

" always has plenty of ,"
ⁿld . "⊙'ll get U some."

☆ted 2 follow . s⟋ped him.
"U poor ," said. " said U
R hungry. ⊙ have some in the yard.

Wh⊙ don't ⊔ eat some."

🐰 went in2 the yard and 8 all of 🐔's 🌱. Then he ran 2 🐭's 🏠. 🐰 was alE there.

"🐰 is hungry," 🐰 was telling 🐭.

"Sleepy 🐱 said he 🪵 give us some 🫐 and 🌾 if ⊙ 🪵 give him some 🥚. 🦆 gave me the 🥚 but she wanted a 🛢. 🐔 gave me a 🛢, but she wanted some 🥤. Do ⊔ have some 🥤 that ⊔ could give me 4 🐔?"

"👁 have plenty of 🥤," 🐭 said. "U 🥫 take all U want and U don't have 2 give me NEthing 4 it."

🐰 gathered a big 🥧le of 🥤. She put it in the 🛢 on 🔺 of the 🎃🎃🎃. She thanked 🐭. Then she 🌸ed the 🛢 2 🐔's 🏠.

🐰 ⭐ted 2 follow 🐰. 🐭 s🔺ped him. "🐰 Ⓜld me U R hungry," 🐭 said. "Eat some 🧀 🐝4 U go."

🐰 8 3 different k👁nds of 🧀 🐝4

he left.

🐞 wanted 2 run 2 catch 🐰.
He wanted 2 tell her that he wasn't
hungry NEmore. But after eating 🍪,
🍿, and 3 k⊙nds of 🧀, it was hard
4 him 2 run. So 🐞 just walked.

B⊙ the t⊙me 🐞 got 2 🐓's 🏠, 🐓
was t⊙ing the fresh 🥛 2 the end of
her 🧹. And 🐰 was gone.

B⊙ the t⊙me 🐞 got 2 🦢's 🏠, 🦢
was setting the 🛢 in the yard 2

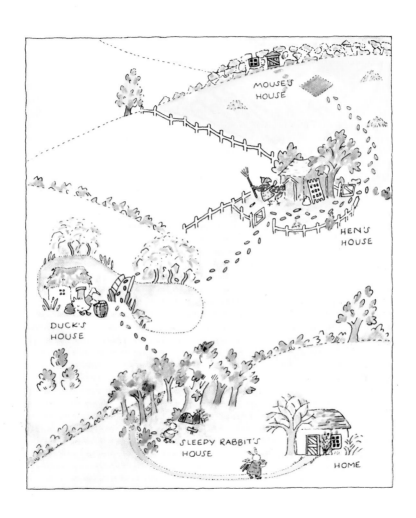

MOUSE'S HOUSE

HEN'S HOUSE

DUCK'S HOUSE

SLEEPY RABBIT'S HOUSE

HOME

catch the ☁. And 🐰 was gone.

B👁 the t👁me 🐰 got 2 Sleepy 🐰's 🏠, Sleepy 🐰 was stuffing his pillow with beans. And 🐰 was gone. But be4 🐰 could leave Sleepy 🐰's 🏠, Sleepy 🐰 s🥕ped him.

"H🥕," Sleepy 🐰 said and gave 🐰 a 🪣 of 🍓🍓. "After U eat the 🥬 and 🥕 that 👁 gave 🐰, U 🥫 eat these."

🐰 was 2 full 2 eat NE of the 🍓🍓 He just carried them 🏠me.

When [picture] got [picture] me, [picture] was alE there. Some [picture] and [picture] were on the [picture].

"Sleepy [picture] gave me [picture] and a big bunch of [picture]," [picture] said. "Now U [picture] sit down and eat."

[picture] looked at the [picture] and [picture]. Then he looked at [picture].

"[picture]'m sorry," [picture] said. "Wh[picture]le U were busy getting me something Z eat, [picture] 8 [picture]. at [picture]'s [picture], [picture] at [picture]'s [picture],

and [cheese] at [mouse]'s [house]. Then Sleepy [rabbit]
gave me a [cup] of [berries], but [eye] was 2
full 2 eat even 1 [strawberry]. And [eye]'m 2 full
2 eat the [turnip] and [carrots]."

"O [deer]," [rabbit] said.

[rabbit] sat down. She looked at the [turnip]
and [carrots] on the [table]. "O [well]," she
sighed. "After all that running around
[eye]'m hungry m[eye]self."

[rabbit] 8 all the [turnips] and a few of the
[carrots]. She put the leftover [carrots] in the

yellow [basket].

"[eye]'m going 2 f[eye]nd a new Ccret place 4 these," she [mouse]ld [rabbit]. "Now close your [eye] [eye]."

[rabbit] closed his [eye] [eye] and [mouse] hid the [basket] under her [bed].

"U [can] o[knife] your [eye] [eye] now," [mouse] said.

She [pick]ed up the [hat] of [berries]. "[eye]'m [skunk] going 2 h[eye]de these [berries]," [mouse] said, "but U R [beaver] 2 eat them. [eye] want 2 give them 2 [mouse] 2 thank her 4 giving

me the 🥤. And so U will 🐛 4get that
they R 4 🐜, 👁 am ma🐌 a 🪧 2
rem👁nd U."

And that's just what  did.

Glossary of Rebuses
and
Bunny Rabbit Story

The rebuses in this
G L O S S A R Y
are in the order that they first appear
in the story.

👁'm = I'm

🐰 = Little Rabbit

📖ld = told

👁 = I

2 = to, too, two

🐰 = Mother Rabbit

4 = for

🐱 = food

🪑 = table

🐰 = bare

🥕 = carrots

h🐰 = here

U = you

C = see

8 = ate

o🖊ed = opened

🐱🌿 = pantry

🚪 = door

🌿 = top

🐱f = shelf

🥬 = lettuce

O = oh

🏮 = well

m👁 = my

Ccret = secret

🐰 = rabbit

cl👁mbed = climbed

🪑 = chair

🍽 = cupboard

🐱h👁nd = behind

🍽🍽🍽 = dishes

🧺 = basket

MT = empty

🐰 = head

E1O = eaten

🕸 = we'll

30

= road	sped = stopped	ished = finished
= house	= would	= roll
= pillow	p = keep	= Mouse
= eyes	le = pile	= dear
= can	l = bowl	$\mathbb{R}$ = are
☆ted = started	= Hen	= corn
w = wait	= barrel	$\mathbb{NE}$thing = anything
d = need	lding = holding	= cheese
= feathers	= not	4 = before
= Duck	= pick	= pail
may = maybe	le = whole	= berries
loo = looking	= bag	me = home
th = think	= seeds	= bed
= rain	ful = mouthful	ma = making
= clouds	$\mathbf{E}$ = ready	= sign
yond = beyond	= straw	
= trees	= broom	

Bunny Rabbit Story

"I'm hungry. I'm hungry," Little Rabbit told his mother. "I want something to eat."

Mother Rabbit looked for some food to give to Little Rabbit. She looked on the table, but the table was bare.

"I thought I had some carrots here," Mother Rabbit said. "Did you see them?"

"I ate them," Little Rabbit told her.

Mother Rabbit opened the pantry door. She looked on the top shelf.

"I was sure I had some lettuce here."

"You did," Little Rabbit said. "But I ate it."

"Oh well," Mother Rabbit said. "I shall look in my secret place. There is always a carrot or two there for a hungry little rabbit."

Mother Rabbit climbed on a chair. She opened the cupboard. She reached behind some dishes and took out a yellow basket. The basket was empty.

"Did you eat these carrots too?" Mother Rabbit asked.

Little Rabbit nodded his head. "I climbed up and found them," he said.

Mother Rabbit got down from the chair. "You've eaten everything," she said. "Well then, we'll just have to get some more. Let's go to Sleepy Rabbit and ask him for some lettuce and carrots."

Mother Rabbit and Little Rabbit walked down the road to Sleepy Rabbit's house. They found Sleepy Rabbit outside, resting on a pillow.

"Who's there?" Sleepy Rabbit asked. He sat up and rubbed his eyes. "Who woke me from my nap?"

"It's me. It's Mother Rabbit. Little Rabbit is hungry. Can you give him some lettuce or carrots to eat?"

"What! First you wake me from my nap. Now you ask me to feed Little Rabbit. Why should I?"

"I'm sorry we woke you," Mother Rabbit said, and she started to leave.

"No. Wait," Sleepy Rabbit called out. "I need something too. My pillow needs more feathers. If you get me some feathers, I'll give Little Rabbit carrots and lettuce."

"Come with me," Mother Rabbit told Little Rabbit. "Let's go to Duck's house. Maybe Duck will give us some feathers."

Mother Rabbit and Little Rabbit walked to Duck's house. Duck was outside, looking up at the sky.

"Do you think it will rain?" Duck asked. "I'm all out of rainwater."

Mother Rabbit and Little Rabbit looked up too. "I see some clouds just beyond the trees," Mother Rabbit said. "It might rain later in the day."

When Duck stopped looking at the sky, Mother Rabbit told her, "Little Rabbit is hungry. Sleepy Rabbit said he would give us some lettuce and carrots if I would give him some feathers. Do you have some feathers that you can give me for Sleepy Rabbit?"

"Take all the feathers you want," Duck said. "They're all over the house. They keep falling out."

Mother Rabbit and Little Rabbit collected a big pile of feathers. They started to leave.

"Wait," Duck called. "Can you get me something to collect rainwater? All I have is this small bowl."

"Hen has an empty barrel," Mother Rabbit said. "Maybe she'll give it to me."

Mother Rabbit ran off to Hen's house. Some of the feathers she was holding flew into the air. Mother Rabbit did not stop to pick them up.

Little Rabbit started to follow his mother.

"Little Rabbit, Little Rabbit," Duck called out. "Don't run off. Mother Rabbit said you were hungry. I have a whole bag of seeds. Why don't you eat some."

Little Rabbit ate one mouthful of seeds after the other. Duck finally stopped him. "You've had enough," she said.

Little Rabbit picked up some of the feathers that had fallen. Then he ran to Hen's house. Mother Rabbit was already there.

Hen was sweeping the floor with a straw broom.

When Hen finished sweeping, Mother Rabbit told Hen, "Little Rabbit is hungry. Sleepy Rabbit said he would give us some lettuce and carrots if I would give him some feathers. Duck gave me the feathers but she wants a barrel. Do you have a barrel that you could give me for Duck?"

"You can take the barrel by the door," Hen said.

Mother Rabbit put the feathers she had inside the barrel. Little Rabbit put the feathers he was holding in the barrel too. Mother Rabbit turned the barrel on its side. She started to roll it away. Hen stopped her.

"Oh Mother Rabbit," she called. "There's something I need. Can you get me some fresh straw for my broom?"

"Mouse always has plenty of straw," Mother Rabbit told Hen. "I'll get you some."

Little Rabbit started to follow Mother Rabbit. Hen stopped him.

"You poor dear," Hen said. "Mother Rabbit said you are hungry. I have some corn in the yard. Why don't you eat some."

Little Rabbit went into the yard and ate all of Hen's corn. Then he ran to Mouse's house. Mother Rabbit was already there.

"Little Rabbit is hungry," Mother Rabbit was telling Mouse. "Sleepy Rabbit said he would give us some lettuce and carrots if I would give him some feathers. Duck gave me the feathers but she wanted a barrel. Hen gave me a barrel, but she wanted some straw. Do you have some straw that you could give me for Hen?"

"I have plenty of straw," Mouse said. "You can take all you want and you don't have to give me anything for it."

Mother Rabbit gathered a big pile of straw. She put it in the barrel on top of the feathers. She thanked Mouse. Then she rolled the barrel to Hen's house.

Little Rabbit started to follow Mother Rabbit. Mouse stopped him.

"Mother Rabbit told me you are hungry," Mouse said. "Eat some cheese before you go."

Little Rabbit ate three different kinds of cheese before he left.

Little Rabbit wanted to run to catch Mother Rabbit. He wanted to tell her that he wasn't hungry anymore. But after eating seeds, corn, and three kinds of cheese, it was hard for him to run. So Little Rabbit just walked.

By the time Little Rabbit got to Hen's house, Hen was tying the fresh straw to the end of her broom. And Mother Rabbit was gone.

By the time Little Rabbit got to Duck's house, Duck was setting the barrel in the yard to catch the rain. And Mother Rabbit was gone.

By the time Little Rabbit got to Sleepy Rabbit's house, Sleepy Rabbit was stuffing his pillow with feathers. And Mother Rabbit was gone. But before Little Rabbit could leave Sleepy Rabbit's house, Sleepy Rabbit stopped him.

"Here," Sleepy Rabbit said and gave Little Rabbit a pail of

berries. "After you eat the lettuce and carrots that I gave Mother Rabbit, you can eat these."

Little Rabbit was too full to eat any of the berries. He just carried them home.

When Little Rabbit got home, Mother Rabbit was already there. Some lettuce and carrots were on the table.

"Sleepy Rabbit gave me lettuce and a big bunch of carrots," Mother Rabbit said. "Now you can sit down and eat."

Little Rabbit looked at the lettuce and carrots. Then he looked at Mother Rabbit.

"I'm sorry," Little Rabbit said. "While you were busy getting me something to eat, I ate seeds at Duck's house, corn at Hen's house, and cheese at Mouse's house. Then Sleepy Rabbit gave me a pail of berries, but I was too full to eat even one berry. And I'm too full to eat the lettuce and carrots."

"Oh dear," Mother Rabbit said.

Mother Rabbit sat down. She looked at the lettuce and carrots on the table. "Oh well," she sighed. "After all that running around I'm hungry myself."

Mother Rabbit ate all the lettuce and a few of the carrots. She put the leftover carrots in the yellow basket.

"I'm going to find a new secret place for these," she told Little Rabbit. "Now close your eyes."

Little Rabbit closed his eyes and Mother Rabbit hid the basket under her bed.

"You can open your eyes now," Mother Rabbit said.

She picked up the pail of berries. "I'm not going to hide these berries," Mother Rabbit said, "but you are not to eat them. I want to give them to Mouse to thank her for giving me the straw. And so you will not forget that they are for Mouse, I am making a sign to remind you."

And that's just what Mother Rabbit did.

CHAPTER 2